AR level 4.6
pts 0.5

Bob White the Quail

David M. Sargent, Jr., and his friends live in Northwest Arkansas. His writing career began in 1995 with a cruel joke being played on his mother. The friends pictured with him are (from left to right), Vera, Buffy, and Mary.

Dave Sargent is a lifelong resident of the small town of Prairie Grove, Arkansas. A fourth-generation dairy farmer, Dave began writing in early December, 1990. He enjoys the outdoors and has a real love for birds and animals.

Bob White the Quail

By

Dave Sargent

Illustrated by
Jane Lenoir

Ozark Publishing, Inc.
P.O. Box 228
Prairie Grove, AR 72753

iii

Library of Congress cataloging-in-publication data

Sargent, Dave, 1941—
Bob White / by Dave Sargent ; illustrated by
Jane Lenoir.
Prairie Grove, AR. : Ozark Pub., 2000
p. cm.
{Fic}21
1567634818 (CB)
1567634826 (PB)
    When Bob White, the father quail, decides it's
time to teach his children how to safely cross a road,
someone else does it for him. Young Amy Armadillo
thinks she can cross a road any ole time she wants and
will not listen to the father quail's suggestions. She
prisses out onto the road and does not bother to look
both ways for traffic. Oh, my! Poor Amy!
Quail -- Fiction.
Armadillo -- Fiction.
Stubborn -- Fiction.
Domestic animals -- Fiction.
Lenoir, Jane, 1950- ill.

Printed in the United States of America

Inspired by

the little covey of quail that live on our farm. We love watching them. Both the mother and father are very protective of their little ones.

Dedicated to

all students who have watched a covey of quail fly up when spooked. We have quail on our farm, and in the spring, when we drive down the road, the mother or father quail will run down the road ahead of us, hoping to lead us away from the chicks.

Foreword

When Bob White, the father quail, decides it's time to teach his children how to safely cross a road, someone else does it for him. Young Amy Armadillo thinks she can cross a road any ole time she wants and will not listen to the father quail's suggestions. She prisses out onto the road and does not bother to look both ways for traffic. Oh, my! Poor Amy!

Contents

Bob White the Quail

If you would like to have an author of The Feather Tale Series visit your school, free of charge, just call 1-800-321-5671 or 1-800-960-3876.

One

Little Miss Priss

The dew on the nearby foliage glistened like diamonds beneath the rays of the bright, early morning sun.

The air felt cool and fresh as Bob White quietly slipped away from the circle of family members who were sleeping peacefully beneath the bush. He ruffled the reddish brown feathers on his small body and cocked his white head from side to side as his eyes scanned the Arkansas countryside for any signs of danger. This is an important day, he thought.

I feel I must teach my children a new lesson on survival.

Bob wriggled his short tail and glanced back at the nest to see if anyone was awake yet. They were still asleep, all in a little circle for warmth and protection.

The father quail yawned and stretched his wings before slowly walking into the big meadow. As a speeding car roared down the country road near Farmer John's place, he tapped one wing on his forehead. "Today I must teach my chicks about all the dangers involved in walking across a busy road!" he exclaimed. "They must learn to watch for traffic at all times."

"Bah!" a young voice shouted. "I'll cross this road anytime I want!"

The unexpected response to his idea surprised Bob. He jumped back and began looking for the scoffer. Seconds later, he saw a little critter slowly shuffling toward him. It had a pointy head, a real skinny tail, and four little short legs protruding from within its bony shell covering.

"And who are you?" Bob asked.

"My name is Amy Armadillo," she replied in a squeaky voice. "And I cross the road anytime I want to go to the other side!"

The father quail looked at the youngster for a moment. Maybe, he thought, I should start my lesson today with a little armadillo student. If I don't educate her on how to cross a road safely, she might have a bad influence on my little ones.

So Bob White cleared his throat, then said to the headstrong armadillo, "Amy, I am a quail, and my name is Bob White. I think you should know that folks traveling on this road or any other road might not see you," he said quietly. "Sometimes cars go too fast. Be careful and make sure the road is safe before you try to cross."

The little armadillo glared at Bob, then shuffled right on past him.

"I have places to go," she said, "and I don't have time to listen to your foolish and unnecessary prattle.

I'm going to visit my cousin who lives on Mr. Brown's farm."

The feathers on Bob White's head stood straight up. "Mr. Brown lives on the other side of the road," he said. "And Amy has not taken one word that I have said seriously!"

He waited, then followed her through the grass. Amid the rustle of her movement, he heard her chanting in a singsong voice.

"I'm going to visit my cousin today. I'll cross that road, and then we'll play. Nobody tells me what not to do. I do what I want, where and when I want to!"

Bob groaned and quickened his pace to catch up with the little rascal before she had a chance to reach the side of the road.

"Wait!" he yelled. "At least let me help you get across safely!"

Amy stopped and turned to face

the quail. She stomped one front foot as though warning him to stay away.

"Please, Amy," the bird pleaded. "Look, I just don't want you to get hurt. I'll watch for traffic and tell you when it's safe to cross."

"No!" young Amy screamed. "You'd just better leave me alone! I've crossed this road to Mr. Brown's lots of times, and I'm going to do it again today, whether you like it or not, Mr. Quail!"

Bob White looked down at the ground and slowly turned around. His shoulders were slumped, and he sighed as he silently began to retrace his steps back to the nest.

Two

Run, Amy! Run!

Bob White felt fear and sadness for the stubborn little girl. But, as he approached the meadow, he heard the familiar voices of his children.

"There's Papa! Good morning, Papa!" they said in unison. "What are you going to teach us today?"

Bob smiled as he hurried toward them. "Today," he said, "I'm going to show you how to cross the road! This is something you will need to know to avoid injury. Folks drive fast sometimes, and they don't have a chance to swerve away from little ones in their path."

The chicks fell in step behind their papa as he turned to leave the nest area. Within minutes, they were near the road. Suddenly, Bob gasped and motioned for his children to halt.

Slow moving Amy Armadillo had finally reached the thoroughfare. She was just stepping onto the road without glancing in either direction. Her gaze was fixed on Mr. Brown's property as she shuffled toward the middle of the paved surface.

Bob White whispered, "Look, my children. That is the wrong way to cross a road. Never cross without looking both ways for traffic!"

"Why, Papa?" one chick asked. "She did, and she's crossing safely."

The daddy quail turned toward the youngster and shook his wing at the little one. "I know that she's crossing safely so far, and has made it without being hit. But," he added, "Amy Armadillo is risking her life in doing it. She is not using good judgment."

Suddenly, Bob heard a noise. His heart pounded as the roar of an engine approached. A second later, his children began to squeal, "Hurry, Amy! A car is coming! Run!"

Bob Quail ran in a small circle, flapping his wings nervously. Amy's life was in danger, but there was nothing he could do. He glanced at his children. Their wings were over their eyes, their bodies trembling.

As the car sped past the little family of quail, the driver swerved to one side. Little Amy's hard-shelled body rolled beneath the wheels.

"Oh no," Bob White groaned as he looked up and down the road to see if more traffic was coming. A truck was approaching from the west. And even though it was traveling much slower, little Amy Armadillo did not try to nor would she have had the time to move out of its path.

The truck moved closer and closer to the still form of the little armadillo. Bob knew she was a gonner. Then, much to his surprise, the truck slowed down and pulled over onto the side of the road. It came to a stop, and the driver got out.

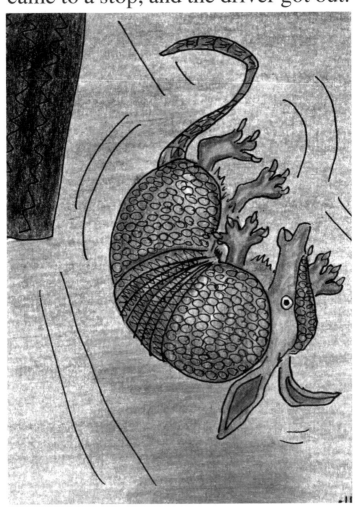

"Farmer John!" Bob gasped. "Children, look! It's Farmer John, and he has stopped to help Amy!"

The man quickly ran to the injured little armadillo and gently picked her up.

"Hasn't anyone ever told you," Farmer John said, "that crossing roads is dangerous? Are you hurt bad, little armadillo? Hmmm, I'll tell you what: I'll take you home with me, and maybe Molly can help you."

Bob watched Farmer John carry the injured armadillo to his truck. He felt a tear trickle down his beak as the kind man laid Amy onto the seat.

A few minutes later, the truck turned down the narrow lane toward the farmhouse and disappeared from Bob's view.

Bob took a deep breath and looked at his children. All four were staring at him, wide-eyed and scared.

"Well, my little ones," he said softly, "I was hoping to teach you about road safety today, and now you have seen a good example of poor judgment. Now, my four little chicks, did you learn anything?"

"Yes, Papa," a chick responded. Amid hiccups and sobs, the others nodded in agreement. "We'll always be careful when we cross a road."

As the youngsters followed their papa toward the nest, one quietly asked, "Will Amy be okay?"

Bob sighed and shook his head. "I honestly don't know," he replied quietly. "I'll take you back to the nest, and then I'll go check on her."

Twenty-five minutes later, Bob rushed into Farmer John's back yard. He quickly hid beneath a bush near the kitchen window, and listened for a medical report on little Amy.

Time passed slowly for the father quail, but he refused to go home to his family until he knew whether Amy was going to be okay. Is she hurt bad? Will she walk and sing and play again? he wondered. Is she even alive? A low groan echoed against the stillness of the evening.

Three

The Bent Tail

Quiet voices woke Bob. He sat up. "Where am I?" he whispered. He ruffled his feathers and flapped his wings. "I should be at home with my family! I should not be here!"

Suddenly, the memory of Amy rolling beneath the car returned to the little bird.

"I must have fallen asleep," he said, as he glanced toward the east.

The sun was peeking over the horizon, casting color across the sky. I must have slept here all night, he thought. And I still don't know the extent of Amy's injuries.

Voices grew louder as the door opened and Farmer John and Molly stepped onto the porch. Molly had a bundle in her arms. She carefully went down the steps to the yard, placed the bundle on the ground and folded back the coverlet.

"There you are, little girl," Molly said with a great big smile. "Do you think you'll be able to walk? Try it. You should be okay now."

    "If," Farmer John added, "you watch for traffic on the road before you attempt to cross it."

    "Whew!" Bob Quail muttered. "The little girl's going to be all right. I'll fly home and tell my children the good news! They'll be so happy!"

Before taking flight, the quail hopped toward the little armadillo. As Farmer John and Molly went back into the house, he whispered, "Amy, are you okay?"

"Y - yes," she replied in a weak voice. "Molly took good care of me. I'm just sore." The armadillo slowly stood up and walked toward Bob.

"I - I am sorry, Mr. Quail, that I didn't listen to your advise," she said. "Your lesson on how to safely cross the road would have saved me a lot of pain and embarrassment."

"Do you have any broken bones?" Bob asked.

Little Amy slowly shook her head. "No broken bones, Mr. Quail," she groaned. "Just bent body parts."

"Which body parts?" the bird asked. "You look pretty good to me."

A tear slid down Amy's cheek as she slowly turned around, exposing a large bandage to the concerned quail.

"My tail, Mr. Quail," she said with a sigh. "The accident bent my tail. Molly said it'll be all right if I'm very careful and keep the bandage in place. I am so ashamed!" she wailed.

The quail looked at the bandage for a few minutes without speaking. Then he smiled. "Well, Amy, you do look a little strange," he muttered. "I'm sorry that you have a bent tail, but it will heal with time."

"Now, Amy Armadillo, you must come home with me and share your lesson on road safety with my chicks. You were a bad example for them, but now your tail will tell more than a thousand words."

Amy nodded her head and fell into step behind Bob White. As the teacher and student moved through the meadow, Bob sighed with relief.

This little armadillo, Bob White thought, will never again cross the road without looking for traffic. She will always be alert when traveling now. Suddenly, Bob stopped walking. She will be a fine example for my little ones.

The quail felt a thud against his back.

"Oomph!" he groaned. "Amy!" he said, "Watch where you're going. You just ran into me!"

Bob White the Quail cocked his head from side to side as though looking for the answer to a puzzle. Amy smiled and blinked one eye. Yes, he decided, she will be careful! Of course she will. Won't she? Hmmm . . .

Four

Quail Facts

The best-known species of quail in the United States is the northern bobwhite, named from the loud call of the male.

The quail is a popular game bird. It was originally a resident east of the Rocky mountains and north to southern Ontario and New England; it has been successfully introduced in parts of western North America, the West Indies and New Zealand. It is 8.5 to 10.5 in long with a slight crest. Males of the northern populations are reddish brown above and white, barred with black, on the belly. The throat and a line above the eye are white; a broad black line extends from the eye backward and around the throat.

This white area is replaced by buff in the otherwise similar females.

In subspecies from the south-western United States and parts of Mexico, the face, throat, and variable amounts of the rest of the underparts are black.

Monogamous, after the breeding season bobwhites gather into coveys-groups that may number over 100 birds, dispersing during the day for feeding. They reassemble at night or in really bad weather. The members of the covey seek both warmth and protection by huddling in a circle, with their heads turned outward.

If frightened, bobwhites (like most quail) will run from danger; when flushed, they fly rapidly with a loud whirring sound, but quickly drop to earth.

BOBWHITE QUAIL

SCALED QUAIL

In the western United States, the most familiar species of quail is the California quail. It is a pretty bird with a recurved black topknot on its head. Its raucous call can be heard in the soundtrack of many Hollywood movies.

A similar species, Gambel's quail, inhabits the deserts of the southwestern United States and northwestern Mexico.

A tropical genus, with fifteen species, contains mostly very dark-colored, solitary birds of the forest floor.

The two species of the south-western United States south to Nicaragua are birds of mountain pine-oak forests. The colorful mountain quail of western North America is also confined to higher altitudes.

Scientific classification: The common quail is classified as *Coturnix coturnix*. The northern bobwhite is classified as *Colinus virginianus*, the California quail as *Callipepla californica*, Gembel's quail as *Callipepla gambelii*, and the mountain quail as *Oreortyx pictus*.